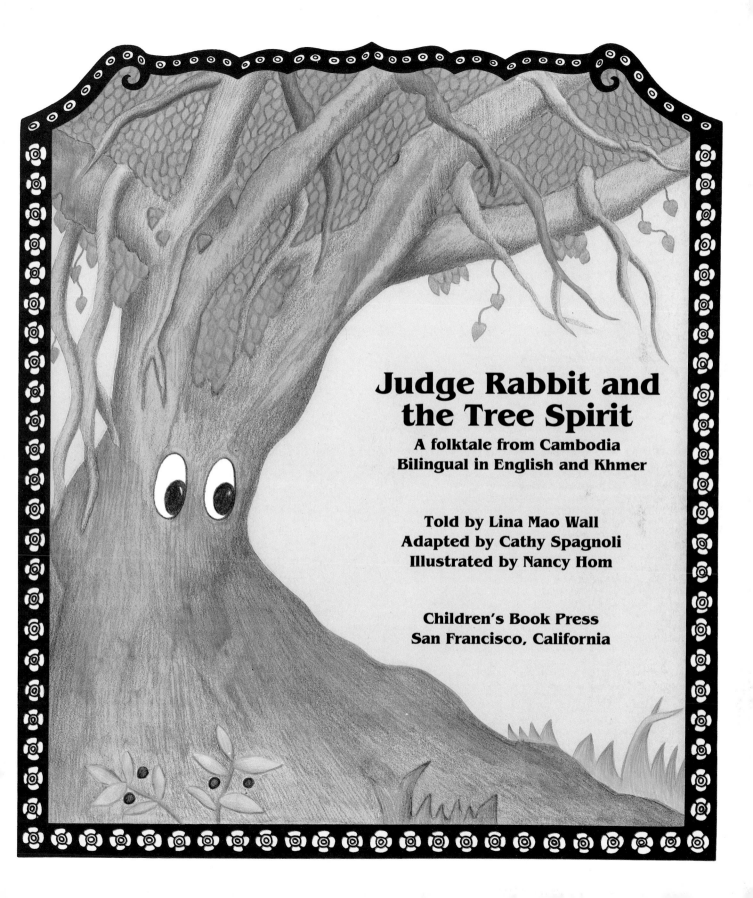

Judge Rabbit and the Tree Spirit

A folktale from Cambodia
Bilingual in English and Khmer

Told by Lina Mao Wall
Adapted by Cathy Spagnoli
Illustrated by Nancy Hom

Children's Book Press
San Francisco, California

Long ago in Cambodia, a young couple sat in peace. Their small house stood a little above the ground, and away from the other houses. In the doorway, the young wife talked shyly to her new husband. Tomorrow there was much work to do, but today they could relax in the warm sunshine.

Just then, in the distance, they heard the sound of drums approaching: TONG! TONG! TONG!

នាសម័យមួយនៅក្នុងប្រទេសខ្មែរ
មានប្ដីប្រពន្ធពីរនាក់
រស់នៅជាច់ស្រយាលពីគេឯងដោយសុខសាន្ត ។
ខ្មួមតូចរបស់គេ សង់ខ្ពស់ពីដីយ៉ាងប្រណិត
ថ្ងៃនេះប្រុសប្ដីប្រពន្ធ កំពុងតែអង្គុយ
លំហែកាយលេខនៅក្រោមខ្មួមក់សត់របស់គេ
ស្រាប់តែសំឡេង ឪ ឪ ឪ សាន់ពួឆ្លៀង ។

The coconut trees seemed to shiver in fright as a messenger from the king suddenly appeared. "Enemy soldiers are coming to take our land!" he cried. "All young men must help in the fight. Follow me now!" He gave the royal orders, then moved on to call others.

"Don't go," pleaded the wife. "We are so happy. Please stay here."

រំពេចនោះ អ្នកនាំសាររបស់ព្រះរាជា
បានមកដល់ផ្ទះបុរសហ្ស៊ីប្រពន្ធដោយមិនដឹងខ្លួន
ហើយក៏បានប្រកាសថា: ប្រទេសយើងមានសត្រួវ
ឈ្លានពាន ព្រះរាជាបញ្ជាអោយអ្នកចូលបម្រើកងឆ័ទ ។

If the king commands, I must go," answered the husband. "I will return as soon as I can."

And so the the wife packed rice with rock salt in banana leaves, and scooped water into a large bamboo tube. She offered the food and water to her husband with a gentle bow. Then she watched sadly as he disappeared into the woods.

ពេលនោះបុរសក៏ពោលឡើងថា៖
បើសិនជាព្រះរាជាបញ្ជារមែនបងត្រូវតែទៅ
ក៏ប៉ុន្តែបងនឹងត្រឡប់មករកអូនវិញ
នៅពេលប្រទេសជាតិយើងបានសុខសាន្ត ។

The husband walked for hours, his sadness following him like a shadow. He thought only of his wife and how much he missed her. At last he stopped to rest beneath a huge banyan tree.

"I can't go on," he said.

Brother Sun was just setting and the heart-shaped leaves of the banyan tree seemed to rattle uneasily. Shadows danced along its roots. Inside this tree lived a spirit—a spirit who now watched the husband.

នៅពេលបុរសចារកចេញដើរកាត់ព្រៃ ព្រោះនៅ
ឧក្សព្រួយបានអន្ទោលតាមគាត់
ដូចជាស្រមោលអន្ទោលតាមព្រាណ
គាត់បានសម្រាកនៅក្រោមម្លប់ពោធិ៍ធំមួយ
ដែលមានបែកសាខាម្លប់ត្រសើ១ត្រសែល ។

I must return to her," cried the husband, and he started back to his wife. Three times he ran towards home; three times he turned away. Inside him, two minds and two hearts struggled, but finally he followed his orders. With a sob, he marched off to war.

"There must be something very special in his house," thought the tree spirit. And he floated off to see what it was.

នៅពេលកំពុងធ្វើដំណើរ បុរសបានគិតថា៖ គាត់ត្រូវតែគ្រប្បប់នៅរក
ប្រពន្ធគាត់វិញ តែចិត្តមួយទៀតគិតថា៖ គាត់ត្រូវតែទៅប់រើជាគិវិញ
គាត់គិតមិនដាច់ស្រេចសោះ គាត់បានគត់គ្រប្បប់នៅគ្រប្បប់មកបី៨
និមផុតគាត់ក៏បានសំរេចចិត្តថា៖ ត្រូវតែទៅប់រើជាគិ ។

When the spirit approached the house he heard sounds of weeping. He saw a beautiful woman with a full moon face, and hair as black as a crow's wing.

"She's sad because her husband left her," thought the spirit. "Well, I know a way to make her happy, and me too." Then the spirit, who could change his shape, made himself look just like her husband.

ផន្លឺញយំសោករបស់នាងជាប្រចាំ បានញុំដល់មិសាចដែលសម្ចំនៅក្បែរផ្ទះ
មិសាចបានឃើញនាងមានរូបនោមលោមពណ៌ល្ពេតខ្មៅ
ទ្ចង់ភ័ក្ត្រមួលក្រឡ្ចងដូចទ្ចង់ខែ ១សក់ខ្នើរលើបដូចស្លាបក្ពែក
ពេលនោះទាក់បានប្រែក្រឡ្ចារអោយដូចប្ពឺនាងបេះបិន ។

Inside the house, the wife heard footsteps coming closer. The door creaked open. She looked out and saw a man standing in the shadows.

"My husband?" she called. "What happened?"

"They didn't need me," the spirit answered in a familiar voice.

"How wonderful," replied the wife. She poured water over his feet to welcome him and he entered.

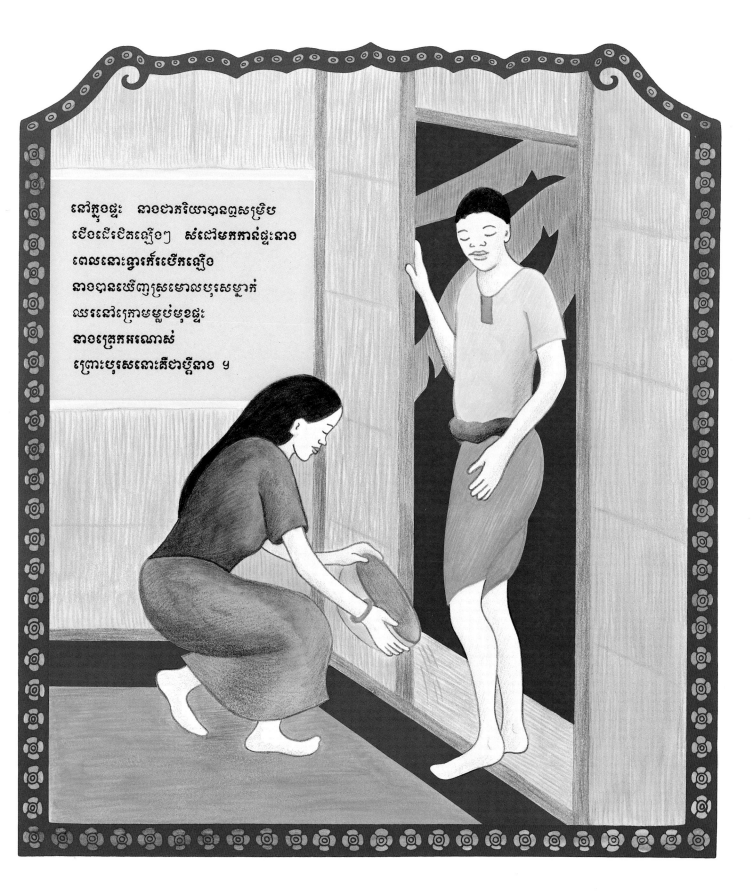

នៅក្នុងផ្ទះ នាងជាភរិយាបានពួសម្រិប ជើងជើរជើតឡើៗ សំដៅមកកាន់ផ្លូវនាង ពេលនោះធ្លាក់របើកឡេ្ទុង នាងបានឃើញស្រមោលបុរសម្នាក់ ឈរនៅក្រោមម្លប់មុខផ្ទះ នាងច្រេកករណាស់ ព្រោះបុរសនោះគឺជាប្តីនាង ។

The next day as always, Sun and his brother Moon flew across the sky. And soon, days and months had come and gone, come and gone.

Every morning the rooster crowed: "KO KAY KEE KOO! KO KAY KEE KOO!" Every morning the wife watched the man walk to his work. But out of her sight, the spirit went right to his banyan tree, for he did not have the strength to stay in disguise all day. Only after sundown could he use his power and become manlike.

នៅលើទេវហាស់ ព្រះអាទិត្យនិងព្រះចន្ទ្រ បានផ្លាស់ប្តូរវេនគ្នាចាំជំនប់
មិនឈ្យរប៉ុន្មានថ្ងៃខែ ក៏បានកន្លងទៅយ៉ាងនាប់រហ័សបំផុត ។
រាល់ព្រឹកព្រលឹម សំឡេងមាន់រទាន គួរអោយស្រណោះ
កុកុទែក គឺគ កុកុទែក គឺគ
ប៉ែណកនាងទេវទែតយគត់មើលប្ដីនាង
ចេញទៅធ្វើការរាល់ៗព្រឹក ។

One evening, the spirit husband returned as usual to the house. A few moments later, the dogs began to bark furiously and the door opened again. In walked the real husband who stopped when he saw—himself, standing near his wife.

"Who are you?" he asked his look-alike.

"I live here. Who are you?" demanded the spirit husband.

"Who is who?" cried the wife. "Why do I see two of you?"

នារាត្រីមួយនោះ បិសាចជាហ្វី បានក្រឡប់មកផ្ទះវិញដូចសព្វដង នៅខាងក្រៅវិញ ជំនោរនារាត្រី និងសំឡេងខ្ញៀរព្រួស លាន់កង្រែង ស្រាប់តែផ្ទាផ្ទះរេបើកឡ្វើង ហើយបុរសជាហ្វីពិតក៏ចូលទៅ តាត់ឈរស្រឡាំងកាំងតែម្ដង ព្រោះតាត់ឃើញ រូបតាត់មួយទៀតឈរនៅរៀបរូបពន្លឆាត់ ។

The wife looked from one to another as they argued. They sounded the same. They looked the same. But she wanted one husband, not two. "Let us go ask the judge what to do," she pleaded, and off they went.

Soon, in front of the village judge, her real husband spoke. "That man is lying. He is trying to steal my wife."

"I do not lie!" shouted the spirit husband. "I am her husband."

នាងជាភរិយា ខំសន្សើងមើលបុរសទាំងពីរ
ដែលកំពុងតែនាស់ប្រកែកគ្នាយ៉ាងខ្លាំង
គេទាំងពីរនាក់ មានសំឡេងនិងមុខមាត់ដូចគ្នាបេះបិទ
តើមួយណាទៅជាប្ដីនាង? នាងត្រូវការប្ដីតែមួយទេ ។

Point to the man you married," ordered the judge.

The wife tried but could not decide.

"If you can't tell," said the judge, "then all three of you must live together."

"Never!" shouted the real husband and he ran off in tears to find help. He stumbled on until he heard a familiar sound: "TCHAAA, TCHAAA, TCHAAA."

ចៅក្រមបានប្រាប់អោយនាងជាករិយា
ចង្អុលទៅបុរសណាម្នាក់ ដែលនាងបានរៀបការជាម្នាក់
តែនាងក៏មិនបានស្គាល់ថា ជាម្នាយអ្នកណាដែរ ។
ចៅក្រមមានប្រសាសន៍ថា៖ បើនាងមិនស្គាល់ថា
អ្នកណាម្នាយជាប្ដីនាងទេ អ្នកទាំងបីត្រូវតែរស់នៅជាម្នាយ ។

It was Judge Rabbit, sitting on a stump munching cucumbers. "What is wrong, friend?" he asked kindly.

The unhappy husband told the rabbit his troubles.

Judge Rabbit scratched his ear. "Don't worry," he said. "Your problem is easy to solve, but you must promise to bring me some sweet bananas, and to keep the dogs from bothering me."

The husband agreed at once and they hurried back to the village.

សុភាននុឡាយកំពុងអង្គុយផ្ចាញ់ពាររុក្ខសក់យ៉ាងរីករាយ ។

លុះឃើញបុរសនោះក៏សួរថា:   លោកបង តើមានការអ្វីរកឹតធ្ងើវ?

បុរសពោលថា:   និងបងសុភាณ์មានព្រះទ័យផ្សារវៃរេអើយ

សូមបងជានៅជួយកាត់សេចក្តីអោយខ្ញុំផង ។

Your honor, I think I know a solution," declared Judge Rabbit with a bow. "I need only a small bottle." It was soon brought and the rabbit held it high. Behind his back, he hid a cork.

"Hmmm, Hmmm," he cleared his throat and straightened his ears. "Here is the test. Only the true husband can fit inside this bottle. The one who lies cannot."

សុភានុឡាយពោលនៅកាន់ទៅក្រម
ដោយលំអោនក្បាលគោរពថា៖
លោកម្ចាស់ ខ្ញុំដឹងថា
ខ្ញុំអាចដោះស្រាយបញ្ហានេះបាន
ខ្ញុំសុំតែកូនជបតុចមួយប៉ុណ្ណោះ ។

The spirit husband smiled in triumph. He could easily enter that bottle. Then the wife would be his forever.

"Let me go first!" he demanded. He made himself like the wind and flowed into the bottle. WHOOOSH!

Judge Rabbit quickly covered the bottle, pushed the cork down, and captured the spirit.

ខណៈនោះមិសាចបានញញញឹមក្នុងចិត្តដោយសប្បាយ ព្រោះដឹងថា
វានឹងអាចប្រែក្លាយចូលក្នុងដបនោះបានដោយស្រួល ហើយវានឹងបានឈ្មុះ
ៗនាងនឹងបានមកជាប្រពន្ធវាវហ្មតជាមិនខាន ។

Take this bottle deep into the woods and throw it far away!" ordered Judge Rabbit.

The grateful couple did as they were told. They took the bottle deep into the woods and then they threw it far, far away. As the bottle fell, a bright streak lit up the night sky. And from then on, the tree spirit never again bothered the wife and her loving husband.

Some say that even today, that ghostly light is sometimes seen at night—to remind us that wisdom can fool even spirits.

សុភាទន្សាយបានប្រាប់ទៅបុរសថាៈ
សូមចោលបិសាចនេះទៅអោយឆ្ងាយ
ដើម្បីអោយដឹងប្រាកដថា
វានឹងលែងមកបៀតបៀនអ្នកឯងបានទៀត ។

About the Story

Judge Rabbit and the Tree Spirit is one of the many Judge Rabbit stories in our Cambodian folktale tradition. The character of Judge Rabbit shows good self-esteem and self-confidence. He believes in himself and his ability to solve problems. He doesn't care how he looks or how little he is compared to other animals. We tell the Judge Rabbit stories to our children at a very young age to encourage them to be self-confident, intelligent, gentle, kind and willing to help others out of their trouble. As Cambodian refugees, we see our children as our hope and our future. I am very excited and thrilled to be a part of making this Judge Rabbit story into a book for children.

Lina Mao Wall

Lina Mao Wall came to the United States in 1983 as a refugee from Cambodia. She now lives in Seattle, Washington where she works as a health services assistant with the Cambodian community. She has also served as the president of the Refugee Women's Alliance (REWA) where she met with storyteller Cathy Spagnoli and members of the Seattle Cambodian community to work on this book.

Cathy Spagnoli, a professional storyteller in Seattle, started to collect stories from Southeast Asian refugees in 1983 as a way to build cross-cultural bridges. This is her second book for Children's Book Press. She previously collaborated with artist Nancy Hom on a Hmong folktale, **Nine-in-One, Grr! Grr!** which was selected as a Notable Book of the Year by the American Library Association and a Cooperative Children's Book Center Choice.

Nancy Hom was born in southern China and grew up in New York City where she graduated from Pratt Institute. She has lived in San Francisco for the past 18 years, where she has achieved recognition for her extraordinary silkscreen art and her dedicated involvement with community arts organizations. She used the media of silkscreen, watercolor and colored pencil for **Judge Rabbit and the Tree Spirit**, her third book with Children's Book Press.

Story copyright (c) 1991 by Cathy Spagnoli. All rights reserved. Illustrations copyright (c) 1991 by Nancy Hom. All rights reserved. Editors: Harrriet Rohmer and David Schecter. Design: Nancy Hom. Production: Alex Torres and Tony Yuen. Printed in China through Marwin Productions. Children's Book Press is a nonprofit community publisher.

Library of Congress Cataloging-in-Publication Data
Spagnoli, Cathy. Judge Rabbit and the tree spirt: a folktale from Cambodia / told by Lina Mao Wall;
adapted by Cathy Spagnoli; illustrated by Nancy Hom. p. cm. English and Khmer.
Summary: Judge Rabbit solves the problem of a mischievous tree spirit who has taken on human form.
ISBN 0-89239-071-9 (lib. bdg.) (1. Folklore—Cambodia. 2. Khmer language material—Bilingual.)
I. Wall, Lina Mao. II. Hom, Nancy, ill. III. Title. PZ8.1.S725Ju 1991
398.24'529322' 09596—dc20   90-26240   CIP AC